W9-AHH-324

Level 1 is ideal for children who have received some initial reading instruction. Stories are told, or subjects are presented, very simply, using a small number of frequently repeated words.

Special features:

Opening pages introduce key story words

Peppa

George

Mr Bull

cave

key

drain

mountain

Large, clear type

Careful match between text and pictures

The mountain is now a cave!

"Daddy helped to dig a big cave!" says Peppa.

Educational Consultant: Geraldine Taylor
Book Banding Consultant: Kate Ruttle

LADYBIRD BOOKS

UK | USA | Canada | Ireland | Australia
India | New Zealand | South Africa

Ladybird Books is part of the Penguin Random House group of companies
whose addresses can be found at global.penguinrandomhouse.com.

www.penguin.co.uk   www.puffin.co.uk   www.ladybird.co.uk

Penguin
Random House
UK

Text adapted from 'Daddy Pig's Lost Keys', first published by Ladybird Books, 2014
This edition published 2018
001

This book copyright © ABD Ltd/Ent. One UK Ltd 2018
Adapted by Katie Woolley

This book is based on the
TV Series 'Peppa Pig'.
'Peppa Pig' is created by
Neville Astley and Mark Baker.
Peppa Pig © Astley Baker Davies Ltd/
Entertainment One UK Ltd 2003.

www.peppapig.com

Printed in China

A CIP catalogue record for this book is
available from the British Library

ISBN: 978-0-241-31255-1

All correspondence to
Ladybird Books
Penguin Random House Children's
80 Strand, London WC2R 0RL

Daddy Pig's Lost Key

Based on the TV series *Peppa Pig*.
Peppa Pig is created by Neville Astley
and Mark Baker

Peppa

George

cave

key

drain

Mr Bull

mountain

Peppa, George, Mummy
Pig and Daddy Pig have
been up a mountain
for the day.

8

Now it is time to go home.

George wants to play with the key.

"George, you must not play with the key," says Daddy Pig.

But then, Daddy Pig
plays with the key.

Daddy Pig has lost
the key. Now it is
down the drain!

"We must go home now,"
says Mummy Pig.

"But I have lost the key,"
says Daddy Pig. "It is
down the drain!"

15

"I can get the key
with this stick,"
says Daddy Pig.

But the drain is too deep!
Daddy Pig cannot get the
key with the stick.

"I can get the key with this rod!" says Daddy Pig.

But Daddy Pig cannot get the key with the rod. The drain is too deep.

"What can we do?" says
Mummy Pig.

Mr Bull has been up the mountain for the day, too. He can help!

"Mr Bull, can you help get the key?" says Daddy Pig.

21

Mr Bull wants to help.
But he cannot get the key.
The drain is too deep.

"What can we do?" says
Daddy Pig.

"We must dig up the
mountain!" says Mr Bull.

Mr Bull digs a cave in the mountain. Now he can get the key!

Mummy Pig, Daddy Pig,
Peppa and George can all
go home.

The mountain is now
a cave!

"Daddy helped to dig a
big cave!" says Peppa.

How much do you remember about
Peppa Pig: Daddy Pig's Lost Key?
Answer these questions and find out!

- Where are Mummy Pig, Daddy Pig, Peppa and George?

- How does Daddy Pig lose his key?

- Why can Daddy Pig not get the key with the rod?

- How does Mr Bull help to get the key?